Dumas: Outrageous

by Eddie J Martin

For: Adrian Byrd, the actor, photographer, artist (painting, drawing, and modeling), and my nephew.

Frederick Dumas

is a different kind of private investigator. At thirty-two years old, he's been around the block. He's five foot eleven, 190 pounds, half Black, half Cuban, with brown eyes, dreadlocks, and a tattoo of his old gang on his right upper arm. Hometown: Miami, Florida.

Up to the age of eighteen, he was the vice president of the Khalifas street gang. He enlisted in the Army for six years, did two tours in Vietnam, was discharged and started working as an understudy with a private investigator. His employer was killed, and he took over the business after finding and taking out his mentor's killers. Dumas found out early on that following the rules hardly ever works, so he hardly ever plays by the rules. Whatever works! Dumas is willing to do whatever he needs to for his clients… up to and including murder.

Chapter One

I shot him in the throat, and he dropped the knife he was attacking me with and grab at his neck and started gurgling. He dropped to his knees and stayed there until I shot him again between the eyes. He fell over head first, still holding his throat.

I took three photos of him and sent them to the number I had on speed dial. Walking out, I passed the two that I had killed earlier and went out the back door. Walked down the street and found a taxi to the downtown area, jumped on a trolley car, and went to the Oktoberfest. Stayed there for two hours and drank four beers and two cognacs. I took a taxi back to my hotel, and at eleven that night, I was on a flight back to the states, Miami Beach, Florida.

Eighteen hours later, I was back in my apartment and in my own bed.

A month earlier, I'd been contacted by a gentleman who had a missing daughter that he wanted me to find. She had been missing for a week, and he guessed she had been abducted.

I asked him, "How did you happen to come up with my name? After all, it's not like I'm a household word, and my office is off the beaten path."

He informed me that he'd been referred by a Mrs. Stone, whom I had done a job for in the past with which she was very happy and had said she'd pass my name around to her friends.

His name was Edward Wynn. CEO of the Wynn medical company. "Are you all that Mrs. Stone says that you are?" he asked?

"That all depends on all that she says I am," I said.

"I mean, do anything or go anyplace if the price is right?"

"My fee is $500 up front plus $200 a day plus expenses."

"Mr. Dumas, I'm prepared to pay you considerably more than that if you can find my daughter."

He went on to tell me his daughter's description: seventeen years old, white, five foot two, 120 pounds, red hair, blue eyes. A tattoo on her right wrist with her name, Jenny. Another tattoo on her left shoulder of a sparrow. "Jenny is very friendly," he said. "Or, she used to be before she was abducted."

"Do you know where she was abducted?"

"All I know is that she was headed to her mother's house – we're separated – to spend the weekend. She never reached there. The police found her car just a mile from the house with everything intact, keys, purse with identification, and money, plus her overnight bag."

"The police haven't come up with anything?"

"They tell me that girls that look like her have been taken before by a group who sold them to the Arabs and shipped them overseas. They say they'll keep searching but give it no chance they'll ever find her. They even suggested that I find someone private."

"How far do you want to take this, Mr. Wynn?"

"As far and as much as it takes – money is no object."

"Okay, Mr. Wynn, I'll need you to send me a check for $10,000, and I'll start right to work on locating her."

And that was how I was hired. The first thing I did was get on the phone to my sources. Otis dabbled in drugs with a group of people who distributed to the street. Otis was always aware of what was going on or knew someone who did. In this case, he knew nothing about abductions, but he did give me a name that I knew very well: José.

José was a local pimp who had over seventy-five girls and was always very protective of them. His girls worked all around the city. He did inform me that not too long ago, a couple of his girls did get abducted, but he knew who was responsible. He had several people working for him; with so many women, he had to. He went to these people who had his girls and demanded them back. One thing led to another, with a couple of killings involved, and eventually the girls were returned.

I told him about the girl I was looking for, and he informed me that if they had her, they wouldn't have her for long. They'd be shipping her out.

"Where do you think I can get that kind of information?" I asked

"I would say from the one who had my girls, but he's no longer with us."

"Anybody else?"

"There may be a fellow who works on the docks. He seemed to be knowledgeable. That's how I found my girls, but it'll cost you."

Ramose was the person he turned me on to, and after a couple of hours trying to locate him, I found out he was off for the day, but I did get his address.

Eight that night, I went over to his house and found the door partly open, so I walked in, calling his name. I heard someone crying in the kitchen, so I walked in there.

Lying on the floor, bleeding from the head, was a man in his thirties and a young woman leaning over him, crying. The woman was in her twenties, slim body and large behind, brunette. I was there for a good minute before she noticed me.

She looked up and saw me and said, "They killed him. He told them he didn't say anything to anyone, but they killed him anyway."

"You knew him?" I asked.

"He's my brother, and they killed him."

"Why did they kill him?" I asked.

"Probably about those girls they were up abducting. He told me all about it. They put them on a ship and shipped them overseas somewhere."

"Why didn't they kill you? They sure wouldn't leave you alive."

"I was in the back room when they came in, and they never saw me. I guess I should call the police?"

"Do you stay here?" I asked.

"No, I have my own place about two miles from here."

"I think you should get out of here. I'll call the police myself. When the police get here, they'll be questioning the hell out of you, and once they find out that you saw the killings, they'll bug you from now on. Then the killers will find out you saw them, and they'll come after you. Save yourself some grief and get the hell out of here."

She stood up, looked at her brother once more, and said, "I guess you're right," and started to leave.

Chapter Two

"By the way," I said. "Did your brother ever mention where they were taking the girls?"

"No, he just mentioned the ships, two of them leaving from his dock every month. One of the ships was named 'Bertha.' You know, he felt bad for those girls, but there was nothing he could do. He was afraid they'd kill him if he said anything; they killed him anyway."

After she left, I checked the place out and called the police, anonymously of course.

I checked the schedule for ships coming in and departing. The Bertha was one of the ones departing in three days. *How in the hell do you check a ship that damn big? Impossible by myself.*

I've heard of cargo ships taking on passengers, maybe Bertha does too. Nothing like finding out. First, I have to find out where the ship is headed, not that it matters. Once I find out where Jenny is, we out of their anyway. Hell, I still don't know if she's going to be aboard that ship, but what I've learned so far is, it's possible.

The next evening, I stopped at LC's, a Mexican restaurant, for a bite to eat. It's not one of my favorite places, but anyplace will do when you just want to fill a hole. At least the margaritas were good.

At the next table sat a beautiful young lady of Cuban descent. Long black hair, face dark and mysterious, earrings, two inches long and gold. Long neck and arms, summer silk dress split up the sides showing long ebony legs. Halter covering melon-sized breasts and open-toed sandals. Her head was down, munching on a salad, except for the times she was looking at me under her eyes.

Hey, I wasn't bad myself. I always pride myself on dressing nice, and I wasn't a half-bad looking guy if I must say so myself.

Five foot eleven, 190 pounds, dark skinned Black man, a gold earring in my left ear, dreads, and wide, black eyes. Eyes that told a story of love and loss and life and death. (A lot of the guys who'd left Vietnam had that same look.)

I wore a silk shirt, open at the neck and down two buttons, pants the same color, and sandals with no socks. I finished my meal and ordered another margarita, and sent my admirer the same. After she received it and the waitress told her who'd sent it, she looked over at me and acknowledge the drink, and I asked if I could join her. She mentioned I could, and I walked over to her table. She looked better up close than she had from where I had been sitting.

"You probably noticed that I've been admiring you. You are a very beautiful lady. I'd love to go to bed with you." The way I feel about it, why waste time on bullshit? She knew and I knew what all this was leading up to… so.

"You don't hold back on your feelings do you? What's your name?"

"Frederick Dumas. You can call me Dumas. And I really would like to go to bed with you."

"Dumas, don't you want to know my name before you jump into bed with me?"

"What's your name?"

"Teresa, Teresa Mongolia."

"Now, how about it, Teresa?"

"How about what, Dumas?"

"Us going to bed together, Teresa? You had more than enough time to think about it."

"Can I finish my drink first?"

Teresa's apartment was off the water in a complex of about twenty other apartments, built around a large swimming pool. She lived on the second floor. Two bedrooms, living area with a small bar. Couch, a couple large lounge chairs, and a cocktail table. The bedroom had one thing I hadn't seen before except in movies, and that was a mirror on the ceiling above the bed. I was increasingly loving Teresa. *I believe the girl is a little bit freaky. We'll see.*

"Well, you've seen it all, Dumas, a couple of bedrooms, the usual. Go over to the bar and pour yourself a drink. I need a few minutes to change."

So I did. After pouring myself a drink, I sat in one of the lounge chairs, put my feet up, and took a hit of the liquor. Ten minutes later, Teresa came out in a sheer white baby Jane nightgown and high heels. The lights were low, but I could see she didn't have on any panties. Once she sat down on the couch and put one foot under her leg, I knew for sure. And then she asked, "Would you pour me a drink? Gin and tonic." I poured the drink and gave it to her.

"Sit here," she said and patted the couch beside her. I sat down with my back at the other end, one knee on the couch and the other foot on the floor, and just looked at her.

We both looked at each other without saying a word, like the bull and the matador. There was no music playing or anything like that; the only thing you could hear was the refrigerator and a few people out in the pool talking about afternoon delight.

Eventually I made it to her side of the couch. Eventually we made it to the bedroom, and at one time during the night, I found myself looking in the mirror on the ceiling.

The night was more than I could have asked for. Loved that mirror.

The next morning, Teresa got up and cooked me breakfast and brought it to the bed. I liked that. Later, as I was about to leave, she asked me if she would ever see me again.

"You damn right," I said. "For the next few days, I'll be out of pocket, but don't you worry. I'll be back."

Outside the apartment, I caught a taxi to my place, and the first thing I did was call the shipping lines and schedule passage on the Bertha, departing at eleven thirty pm that next night. The Bertha's destinations were Jamaica, Hamburg, Germany, Korea, Japan, and Hong Kong. I told them that I wanted to take the round trip and back home again. They said the trip would take six to eight weeks. I hoped it wouldn't take me that long to find Jenny. I sure didn't want to be away from Teresa any longer then I had to.

Chapter Three

The next night, waiting outside my apartment for my taxi, bags by my side, a teenager was passing by, pants hanging down below his ass and needing a haircut. T-shirt with "Long Live Elvis." Tattoos going up his arm and covering half of his face. After he got around six to ten feet past me, he stopped very quickly, turned around, and held a knife to me and said, "Give me all your money. And I'll be taken those bags too."

"You sure you want to do this, my man?" I said.

"Shut the fuck up and give it up. You don't need it nohow."

"Give me a chance to give you my wallet in my back pocket," I said, and I reached into my left back pocket. I keep my wallet in my right.

What I pulled out was not my wallet but a two-shot twenty-two derringer and immediately shot him in his left knee. He screamed and dropped the knife, fell to his good knee on the ground, moaning, and looked up at me as if to say, "You didn't have to do that!"

I started to shoot him again in his other knee, but I didn't. I just kicked him in the face. I think I broke his nose. I know I kicked out a couple of front teeth. After, he fell flat on the ground, and I kicked him a couple more times. He crawled away, crying and moaning, a good thing too because that was when my taxi rolled up.

I checked in at the Bertha with thirty minutes to spare. They put me in a nice little cabin with a bath plus shower, bed, and writing table. There were four other passengers besides me: a retired doctor and his wife, Mr. and Mrs. Elmore, a middle-age writer on vacation, Calvin Howard, and a thirty-something female who just wanted to get away from it all, or so she said, a Ms. Clara Edmonds.

Eleven thirty-five, the Bertha cast off, and we were underway. We all were on deck, watching the sendoff; no one was watching us back. Two of the rooms were one deck down, and two were on the upper deck. Mine and the teachers were below deck. On the back of the door, inside the room, were emergency procedures and mealtimes. Three meals a day, seven, twelve, and five. There would be snacks available in the mess hall anytime.

At breakfast the next day, we all introduced ourselves to one another. The doctor and his wife were in their mid-seventies, and he was a retired general practitioner. They were on the cruise to see the world, and this was the cheapest way. Slow and easy, that's what they liked, and there was not a lot of people to share the ship with.

The writer had time off from teaching history at the University of Ohio to write a book, and he felt this was a good way to do it.

The next was Ms. Clara Edmonds, five foot four, 110 pounds, slim, with a very strange face. Long straight nose and chin, She seemed like a typical Caucasian from Illinois to me. She was young but carried herself as though she were much older. Very quiet and stayed to herself quite a bit. I only saw her at mealtimes and sometimes on deck. Never did find out her story. I tried. Of course, I was the only black passenger on board, excluding the crew. They were of all nationalities.

The captain was cool. He would join us for supper and chat casually about things I didn't care about that much, but I had to listen. Breakfast and lunch, we were on our own.

It was time that I started looking for Jenny, and a couple of days out I did just that. There were five decks to the ship. I figured I could eliminate the main deck, so I started on my deck, deck two. There were two rooms I was sure of that were empty. I was in one, and the writer the other. The others were for utilities, etc.

I tried the third deck and found only the radio room and crew quarters. In the hallway, one of the men spotted me and asked what I was doing down there.

"I'm just looking around," I said. "Got bored staying in my cabin. I notice you guys got a little craps game going on. Can anybody join?"

The guy looked at me and noticed that I was one of them. "Sure, why not," he said.

I followed him into the room, and there were four other crew members shooting craps off the floor on a blanket.

"New player," the person I'd followed into the room said.

They all looked up at me. Most I'd seen on deck and had spoken to, things like "Hey, brother, what it is?" Street talk. So they were at ease with me already.

"Hey, man what you know? You got tired of your cabin already? one said. "Come on in. Your money is good here."

So, for the next three hours, I was down on my knees, tossing the bones around. Lost about seventy-five dollars, which wasn't bad, and quit about midnight. The crew didn't talk about anything other than the expected storm and the ship's condition, plus the lady on the first deck. They asked me about her and what I could tell them. I told them what I knew, which was nothing, really.

"Strange lady," one of them said, "but we do get some bizarre people taking this voyage. Remember the guy in cabin three about a year ago? That's your cabin, Dumas. He used to stay in his cabin like that, never would come out except for meals. A cruiser stopped us in the middle of the ocean and took his ass off. We were in international waters. But man, did they have the heat, including a couple of deck guns. He begged the captain not to let them take him, but there was nothing the captain could do. He was concerned more about his ship and the crew. Never saw the guy again."

On the way to my cabin, I decided to go up on deck and get some air. Ms. Edmonds was there with a shawl wrapped around her shoulders. It was a bit cool.

"Good evening, Ms. Edmonds," I said. "Couldn't sleep?"

"No," she said. "I thought maybe a little air might help."

"If that don't do it, I think I saw some brandy in the mess hall."

"Thank you, Mr. Dumas, but I have brandy in my cabin already." And then she said, "Good night, Mr. Dumas."

Chapter Four

The next morning, after breakfast, I went to visit the captain up on the bridge. From there, you could see the entire ship: the containers up front, ten high and thirty across, and the door that opened to the lower deck, where cargo was also stored. The captain told me that at each stop, they would drop off and pick up cargo. Their average time stopped was approximately two to three days.

I got the feel of what a cargo ship does. One of the crew members came in and started talking about some women and how one was hysterical. He never noticed me until the captain put up his hand to stop him and pointed at me. I had my back to them, looking out the window, but I could still see them through the glare in the glass. The crewman made a beeline back out the door. Naturally, I acted like I hadn't heard a thing.

After a minute or so, the captain asked me "Why are you taking this trip?"

I informed him that things had gotten a little hot around Miami, so I'd thought it best if I left town for a while. "When people are looking for you, they hardly ever look at a cargo ship. They're looking at the train stations, airlines, or bus stations. I started to try and hire on, but that would have taken too long."

"Hell, Mr. Dumas, if you needed a job, I could have taken you on without papers."

"Captain, I'm going to be with you the whole trip, so I still may need that job."

When I left the bridge and the captain, I had a good idea that the girls were aboard the ship, but I wouldn't be able to do anything until we got to another port. It was a good bet the whole crew was in on the scheme; I'd assume they were anyway.

Lunch always surprised me. You wouldn't think that of a cargo ship, although breakfast and dinner weren't bad either. Friday nights, they had steak, and you cooked your own on the grill. Everything else was laid out for you.

The weekends were kind of laid-back, with cold cuts, shrimp, and whatever they kept in the freezer.

Saturday afternoon, after lunch, one of the crewmen saw me on deck and said there was a game later that night. "Come on down. And by the way," he said, "there's also going to be a poker game."

The writer came up to me and said, "I see you're getting to know the crew? You think that's wise?"

"Just a way to pass some time, Mr. Howard. After all, people are people. You should know that. How's the book coming?"

"I've been stuck for the last couple of days. It happens to me sometimes. By the time this trip is over, I hope to have it finished."
"And if not?" I said?

"I'll go around again, maybe stop off at one of the islands. Hey, what's with Miss Edmonds? You ever get a chance to talk to her, other than meals, I mean?"

"No," I said. "Every time I tried talking to her she cut the conversation short. Maybe she doesn't like men."

"I thought about stopping by her cabin one night, but didn't. There's something about her that tells me to keep away. Know what I mean?"

I told him I did, and he continued walking on, around the deck.

The Elmores were in lounging chairs, reading books. They seemed to be taking this trip for what it was… a vacation.

Later, they walked the decks. I even saw them up in the bridge, visiting with the captain, and afterwards, I saw the elder Mr. Elmore walking around on the second deck. He said what I said: "Just browsing." I noticed Mrs. Elmore around the containers and wondered what she was doing there. Just browsing, I guess.

That night, I walked into the area the games were going on in. It was on the third deck. Five guys were on their knees, shooting dice, two sets of them. There was a poker table, with four sitting and playing, and what looked like a blackjack table.

In the crew, they employed four women: one white, one Cuban, one Black, and a Mexican. All were positioned in one spot or the other. I guessed they'd hired the different nationalities to adhere to the hiring policy. A couple didn't look too bad, but they sure talked as much shit as the men. I guessed they would have to, the type of work they performed. No office duties here.

I squeezed between two men in one of the craps games and made my bets. Later that night, I went from the craps game to the poker table. With all that gambling, you just knew somebody had to have alcohol that they shouldn't have, that they were selling.

Once the captain passed by, that told me this was nothing new, that they'd done this before. My luck was going well there for a while until about the fifth hand. I was going to go back over to the craps game before it turned.

Seven card draw… My first three cards were two queens in the hole and one up. Looking damn good already. I looked around the table, and the only card I saw that was higher than mine was a king. I thought, *I've got the best hand so far, and I may pull in this pot.*

The bet went down; the cards were dealt.

The first player received a four to go along with his ten of hearts. He folded.

The second player received a jack of hearts to go along with his deuce of hearts.

The third player received a seven of spades to go along with his deuce of clubs.

The fourth player had folded before the bet.

That left me, and I received a four of diamonds to go along with my queen.

Next bet, everyone checked. I bet. Everyone but the first player called. The dealer dealt the cards.

The first player had folded.

The next player received another jack, giving him a pair.

The third player received a second seven of clubs, giving him a pair. I was next and received a four of diamonds, giving me a full house, three queens and two fours. I felt good then. I felt the pot was mine. Two more cards to go.

We bet, and the dealer dealt the last card, and it was dealt down.

The jacks bet. I raised him, and the sevens raised me.

The jacks bet again. I raised him again, and the sevens raised both of us.

The jacks looked at both of us, our hands and then our faces. I had a queen and a pair of fours showing, plus a six of clubs. The other player had a pair of sevens showing and two lesser cards, nothing, really. I felt that the most the jacks had was a full house, jacks high.

So, the only one I had to fear was the sevens. *What could he have going along with those sevens?*

The jacks bet, I raised him, and the sevens raised us both.

We both called.

The jacks showed his hand first, three jacks and two deuces.

I was next, with my three queens and two fours. I was ready to pull in the pot.

The guy with the sevens was next, and he moved the two sevens aside by themselves, and out of the hole, he brought two more, four sevens.

I was sick. The guy with the jacks fell back in his chair and onto the floor. The person with the sevens laughed and pulled in the pot. A very nice pot if I must say so myself.

Chapter Five

I told them right after that hand that I had to take a break. They all understood. I took my drink, walked outside the room, and sat on some steps nearby. Ten minutes after I had sat down, one of the crew members passed me from the back of the ship, went into the game room, and came back out with Sydney, one of the guys I knew as a crew boss. He was telling him, "The first thing I heard was the girl screaming, and I ran into the room, and there was Ken trying to rip the girl's clothes off. We stopped him, but not before she went hysterical."

"I warned Ken about this shit before. No one wants these girls if they're all fucked up. Hold him where he is, and I'll see what the captain wants to do with him."

I was up on the steps in the shadows, and they never saw me. I followed them to the back of the ship, past the cargo area; there was another room or two back there.

Seymour went into one of the rooms, and I could hear a girl crying and Seymour saying, "Are you all right? Did he molest you?" The answer, between sobs, was no. "That'll never happen again," Seymour said. "I promise."

When the door opened, I did get a glance into the room. It looked like at least three to four other girls were in there.

Seymour came out and walked over to another room, but before he did that, he made a call. He walked into the room, and I heard two or three sharp sounds that sounded like slaps and Seymour saying, "Ken, I've warned you about this shit before. I've told you."

They both grabbed Ken by his arms and took him toward the back of the ship, where there was a door leading to the outside. Ken tried to struggle but was too drunk to make any difference. All I could hear him say was, "No, no, please."

I made it back to the game and my seat at the poker table.

The next morning, things went on as usual: breakfast, lunch, and dinner; the passengers doing their thing, strolling the deck, laying around, reading books, and napping; the crew doing their thing. I never did see Ken again; if I had to guess, I'd say he was food for the fish by then.

Our first port of entry was Jamaica. We put in anchor a half-mile off for a day until they had room for us to unload at the dock. Once there, the men started unloading and loading the cargo for the next stop. Of course, we did get to stay in Jamaica a few nights.

I got a chance to go down to the cargo area where the girls were. There was a guard near the door, holding an M-16 rifle. No chance of doing anything here. I did notice that the cook was sending down meals on trays, seven of them. In the mess hall, we never saw any of this. Probably happened before or after meals.

Meanwhile, in the women's quarters were seven women, all white, blonde, and blue-eyed except for one, a four foot eight Chinese-American. She looked exactly like a doll. She was beautiful. She was the same individual that Ken had tried to rape. She was still in a hysterical state, and the other girls tried their best to calm her down, but to no avail. Behind the women's cabin was a door leading out onto a deck behind the ship. During the time in port, that door was always locked, but once they got on the high seas, it was open so they could go out and get much-needed air.

Once we left Jamaica and were a day out, one of the crew members unlocked the girl's door. A few of the girls went out on the deck to sun themselves. The Chinese doll was the last one to go out. She sat down on one of the lounge chairs and just stared at the swell behind the ship. After a couple of hours, a few of the girls went back in, when it came time for the doll, she stood up, walked over to the rail, and before anyone could stop her, climbed up and jumped over. All the girls started shouting and screaming and informed their guard. He, in turn, notified the captain. They asked the captain to stop the ship and go back for her, but he refused, saying, "There are sharks that follow the ship. Even if we did stop, there is no chance we'd ever find her alive. There goes over $100,000 I just lost."

After a few days, things were back to normal. The girls had just about forgotten the Chinese doll, and the games continued as usual. Of course, the passengers knew nothing of the incident, but I knew. And I was just waiting for my chance.

I still didn't know if Jenny was aboard or not because I hadn't seen her. My bet was that she was.

One day, I asked Seymour where Ken was, saying that I hadn't seen him in a while. Of course, I already knew; I just wanted to hear what he'd say.

"Oh, he got off the ship in Jamaica and never returned. Met a woman, I'd bet. He's always doing shit like that. Can't keep his hands off the ladies.

Later, I was contemplating how to get Jenny and the girls off the ship, but I didn't want to be like Ken (fish bait), so I knew that was out. Anything I did would have to be at one of the next posts. I had a feeling that Hong Kong or some Asian port would be most likely.

A few days later, the captain called me up to the bridge.

"Dumas," he said. "I've been watching you and noticed that you seem to get along with the crew well. About that talk we had a while back about you maybe needing or wanting a job, are you still thinking in those terms?"

"Are you offering me a job, Captain?"

"It appears we're missing a man, and since you showed interest in a job, right away, I thought of you," the captain said. "It's hard to get a replacement out here on these waters."

"Where would I be working?" I said.

"I'll start you off in the kitchen and then later move you someplace else. I heard you talking to the crew about Vietnam. Were you ever there?"

"I did two tours there in the Mekong Delta. I was an Army scout."

"Did you do any drugs or anything else like that while you were there?"

"Sure, I did. That's the only way a lot of us made it through. You must remember we were dealing with the jungle and all that entails, plus the Vietcong were trying to kill us. I have no apology for that."

"I understand there were a lot of drugs being sold and transported out of the country. Is that true?"

"Probably so, but I would have no knowledge of that. Where I was at, we couldn't even get a beer. That's why so many of us were on drugs."

"Were you ever running drugs?"

"I plead the fifth on that, Captain."

"Think about my offer, Mr. Dumas. We do need someone in the kitchen, and the pay is not bad."

I did think about the offer, the pros and the cons. *If I start working in the kitchen, it will give me more excuses to survey the ship. Besides playing poker and craps with the crew, I may be able to make contact with the girls. Right now, I have no reason to be wandering around unless I'm part of the crew. We've got another four weeks to be out here, and that would give me plenty of time to find Jenny and the rest of the girls if I'm lucky.*

So, I went to work in the kitchen. For a while, my job was basically washing dishes. Some would think that it was beneath me (my passengers did), but what they didn't know was that I had served in the military and I'd had many days at KP, so this was nothing to me, plus the pay was good.

Chapter Six

After about a week of KP, they were comfortable with me, and I got promoted. Now I was a server of the meals, and someone else did the dishes. Well, the only ones who had dishes were the passengers; the rest of us had trays.

One afternoon, I went below deck to my room and saw something I thought was very strange. Ms. Edmonds was having a conversation with the captain. I hadn't seen that before; she'd hardly ever left her cabin or the first deck. *I've seen those who go talk to him, but it's usually on the bridge. Now, what could that be all about?* I went on into my cabin, closed the door, and tried to listen through it, but no chance. But I did notice her shaking her finger at him, and that was very strange. I'd never seen a passenger shake their finger at the captain before.

The writer got sick and couldn't leave his cabin, so we, I mean me, had to take his meals to him. It wasn't so bad. I got a chance to shoot the shit with him, asked him how his book was coming. He told me Mr. and Mrs. Elmore had looked in on him, but not Ms. Edmonds. "I guess she's been too busy," he said. "Even a couple of the crew stopped by."

There must have been something going around because a few of the crew caught it, and they were laid up for a while too. The good doctor ended up helping the ship's doctor. One of those who'd gotten sick was a kitchen helper, and that put us short, so short that not only was I delivering meals to the writer, but to the lower deck and the girls. I wasn't allowed to take the meals to the girls in their rooms; I just left them outside the door, and the guard would come along and open it. *Well, I'm getting closer*, I thought. *Six trays, used to be seven.*

The next port was Lisbon; the same thing happened there, except a storm kept us there a few extra days. Most of the men went into town. To make it look good, I went in overnight but came back early.

The girls stayed locked up, and the cook asked me to deliver their noon meal. When I got down to their cabin, the guard was over in the corner, throwing up, holding his stomach, and moaning. His M-16 was lying on the floor beside him. I asked him, "Is there anything I can do?"

He replied, "No. I guess I just got what everyone else has. Damn, I can't even move."

"Well, look," I said. "I have the girls' food. Can you open the door?"

"Hell no," he said. "Does it look like I can open any damn door? Here." And he handed me the keys.

I took the keys and unlocked the girls' door. He lay back down on the floor, still moaning. I took the trays inside the room, and for the first time, I saw the girls all together. To me, they all looked alike: blonde, blue-eyed, etc. As they were taking their trays, I said to each one, "Jenny."

The fourth one said, "How do you know my name? I haven't seen you around here before."

"Just a lucky guess," I said.

I'd never expected this, so I didn't have a plan. Off the top of my head, I thought, *We're tied up to port; why not get out of here? But then we're on the bottom deck. They still have crew members around. Swim, if the girls could swim. I've got the key to the back deck. Why not.*

The guard called out in a loud voice, moaning. I told the girls I'd be back and asked if they all could swim.

I went out of the room, closed the door, went over to the guard, and helped him up and to his quarters.

I made it up to my cabin, retrieved my .38 and derringer, placed it in a plastic bag, and headed back to the lower deck and the girls. Once there, I opened the back door and herded the girls out onto the deck. The dock wasn't far, and if the girls could swim at all, they'd make it with no problem. I instructed the girls to go up from the ship once out of the water and that then they were on their own to go find a policeman or something, just get the hell away from the ship. The water was about twenty feet down from the deck. Once I told them to hit it, some jumped and some even dived in; they were just that damn good. Jenny and I were the last to go, and once we hit the water, she nearly outswam me.

Once we made it to the dock, the other girls were nowhere in sight. Down the dock, we located a truck with the keys in it and jumped in. Further on up the road, we saw two of the girls. We stopped and picked them up and continued. Looking up at the sky, one of the girls noticed an airplane headed for an airport. It looked like it was getting ready to land, so we followed it.

We made it to the airport, and the first thing I did was call Mr. Wynn. I informed him that I had his daughter and needed transportation quick. He said he'd get a charter plane and to stay by the phone. Ten minutes later, he told us where to go, but first, he wanted to speak with his daughter.

Forty-five minutes later, we were on a jet with a cool drink in our hands, headed for home. It was only then that I thought about the other three girls, and I hoped they'd made it.

I found out that the other two girls had wealthy families and they could talk to them while on the plane. The girls told their people what had happened and who'd rescued them. Their people told them that they would reward me. One of the girls already had a $100,000 reward for her return.

Chapter Seven

"Captain, the girls are gone, the cabin is empty, and the door to the deck is open," said a crew member who was relieving the last guard.

"What do you mean the girls are gone?" Don't tell me that."

"I'm afraid so, sir. They're gone."

"I'll be right down, and this better be a joke."

The captain ran down to the lower deck and the girls' cabin. The guard was there in the doorway, guarding an empty room.

"What happened?" said the captain. "How did they get loose? Who let this happen? Where is everybody?"

"Most of the crew is out sick or in town. The guard, I believe, is in his bunk, sick."

"Where is Seymour? Is he around?"

"No, sir, he's still in town."

"Get everyone that's on board and find those girls, right now."

More than half the crew was in town, and the others were in bed sick. The head cook came to the captain and said that he couldn't find Dumas. "The last time I saw him, he was taking dinner down to the girls."

The captain went to the quarters of the last guard; he was sick as hell, but he managed to tell the captain that he'd given Dumas the keys before Dumas had helped him back to his bunk.

The captain could only round up a fourth of the crew before it was over. Later, the rest of the crew started showing up, and they were sent right back out to search for the girls.

The captain figured that the girls had at least three to four hours' head start, but without any money, they wouldn't get far.

Ms. Edmonds found the captain in his cabin and asked him directly, "Captain, what's this I hear about our cargo having left the ship? You do realize that's my shipment and is worth some $5 million to me and, I might add, $700,000 to you; now, what are you doing to get them back?"

"I've got the men out looking for them right now. It shouldn't take long."

"I hear Dumas is with them? That right? Did he help them?"

"I don't know that yet, but we can't locate him. It's safe to say he may be involved and set them free."

The next day, Seymour called and gave the captain the bad news. "They followed one of the girls to the police station, and they, in turn, called her country's consulate. She's in their hands now.

"A couple of the crew caught up with one of the girls in the marketplace, grabbed her, and was about to bring her back to the ship when she started screaming, and the people at the market jumped on them, beat the hell out of them, and the girl got away. They are in the local hospital right now. We'll need to get replacements for them. One other girl got a ride on a fishing boat to another island, and from there, who knows.

"One other thing, we traced the other three girls to the airport, and they caught a chartered flight from there. And Captain, Dumas was with them."

"Are you leaving us, Ms. Edmonds?"

"I'm afraid so, Captain. There is nothing else I can do here. You let my cargo escape, and as you know, that's the only reason I was here. You've lost me a lot of money, me and my investors. You'll have to pay for that, Captain."

"Would resigning help the situation any, Ms. Edmonds?"

"I don't think so, Captain. We lost close to $10 million losing those girls, plus the delivery to our customers. They're waiting for those girls, who will never arrive. So no, Captain, resignation won't do it. Your next port will be Hong Kong. It would be best if you didn't go there. Do you get my meaning?"

"You can't be serious; shipping is my whole life. Look, Ms. Edmonds, can't there be another way?"

"Well, you could explain what happened to the Arabs. I'm sure they'll want to hear all that from you. Then they'll torture you, and then they'll kill you. I'll be going back to the States."

"What should I do? This is my life?"

"There is room on the flight back to the States," she suggested.

"No, I have too much to lose. After all, they haven't paid us yet. How bad could it be? I think I'll take my chances."

"It's your skin, Captain."

Seymour joined the captain on the deck and said, "I guess Ms. Edmonds is pissed off?"

"Wouldn't you be? She just lost close to $10 million on that shipment, and I hate to tell you this, but the crew has lost quite a bit too."

"Did she threaten you, Captain?"

"You could say that she advised me to run because the Arabs won't take too kindly to me losing their merchandise."

So, what are you going to do?" Seymour asked.

"The Arabs haven't paid us, so they haven't lost anything, but then, she might be right, that might make no difference to them. You know they like to torture people for little or no reason. I'll be taking a chance if I pull into port, but what choice do I have? This ship is my life."

"Maybe you could call them and tell them what happened and get a feel on how they take it?"

"They will just lie until I get to the port and then put the screws to me," the captain said. "I've got enough money so that I could quit right now, but that half a mill would have come in right nicely."

"You're right about that, Captain; I was sure looking forward to my share."

"How could I have been that wrong about someone? Dumas fooled the hell out of me. All the girls, he got all the girls out without a shot being fired."

"Captain, you're not alone. He fooled all of us, and we spent the most time with him. Playing poker, shooting dice, that's when you get to know someone. We were wrong, and it cost us. Dumas, is that even his real name? I'll bet not. He wouldn't tell you his real name, would he?"

"I don't know, Seymour, but I do know one thing. Mr. Dumas needs to be dead. There is no doubt about it. Once we get out of this mess with the Arabs, we must make it so."

Thirty-eight thousand feet over the ocean, the last part of the trip to the States, I was stretched out and thinking over the last couple of weeks. Overall, it hadn't gone bad; I figured I'd only lost one girl (the doll), but that hadn't been my fault. I'd gotten three girls out safely and another three away from the ship, all without a shot being fired.

Things had fallen into place for me: the storm, the crew getting sick, and the men being in town, getting laid. Yes, everything had fallen into place.

With the money I've made off this caper, I'll be able to retire, but who retires at thirty-four?

I was thinking about buying a new car, since I didn't have one. *That would be nice. But then again, they're a lot of trouble, plus Miami has a lot of traffic, then I'd have to buy insurance, and then there is the upkeep. Who needs it?*

Chapter Eight

A new office would also be nice, but then, people seem to find me where I'm at. I'm off the beaten path, but that's all right.

What about a secretary? She could answer my phone calls, take my messages, and type my letters. Bring me coffee. No, it would be more trouble than it's worth. I'd also have to pay her… I think I'll just keep my ass where it is, here, "alone."

My girl, Teresa, wasn't too far off my mind, and I thought later that night I would check her out. First, I'd go over to the Seafront restaurant on the beach for some seafood. I had a taste for some oysters, shrimp, and lobster, with scallops on the side. *I haven't had a mai tai in a while now. That would surely be nice.*

I called a cab, and fifteen minutes later, I was at the beach in front of the Seafront restaurant, a two-story bamboo building half overlooking the water, with a patio going all around the place. I got there at a good time, right after the noon crowd and right before the evening meal. I figured I'd make it to Teresa's about nine that night, after I rested up, and we could either go out to dinner or not, probably not.

I walked up the stairs to the second floor, and at the top, you could either go left or right. Left was toward the water side. Right was looking down on the beach. I grabbed a table by one of the open windows and gazed at the horizon as I ordered my mai tai and seafood platter. I turned my gaze to the interior of the restaurant. A small crowd was there, couples and foursomes in swim gear, a few businessmen discussing business over a drink.

The restaurant was open on four sides, and there was a nice breeze flowing through the building, and after eating, I sat back, stretched out, and ordered another mai tai. I happened to glance over at the steps, and there, about to walk down the stairs, was Teresa. When I spotted her, she saw me at the same time, and we locked eyes. That should have been a magical moment except for the guy that was holding her arm to walk down the stairs. When she saw me, she stopped, and the person with her looked at her and where she was looking and spoke to her. She didn't answer him but walked on down the stairs.

Well, I'll be damned, I thought. *Never know what you'll see in Miami. The night I had planned just walked down the stairs. It's only been three weeks. Didn't take her long to move on. Oh, well, what the hell, another one bites the dust.*

The next morning, I woke up in my apartment with a headache you wouldn't believe. Somewhere along the way, I'd switch from mai ties to vodka and then to tequila. The room was spinning, so I didn't attempt to get up, just closed my eyes, and even that was hard to do. I looked over at the clock and it read ten fifteen. I didn't know whether that was am or pm. I assumed it was am. After ten minutes, or so, I put one foot out the bed and then waited two minutes and put the other one out. I walked to the bathroom and took care of business and jumped into the shower. I let the cool water flow over me first for at least ten minutes, then the hot, and then the cool again. I dried off, wrapped a towel around myself, and walked into my kitchenette, which isn't far from my bedroom because they're both the same. You see, I lived above a coffee shop, my office apartment all in one, office in one room with separate doors for my living quarters. There was a door that led to my office from my apartment, and separate doors from the outside that led to both.

It was a small kitchenette with two burners and small coffee pot that brews two cups at a time. Not much, but I like it. Plus, I get to smell freshly brewed coffee all day from the shop below; that is, whenever I'm there. While the coffee was brewing, I put my drawers, pants, and T-shirt on, walked into my office area, which consisted of one large desk, one small couch, and one lounger and chair in front of my desk. I figured I should have one thing nice in the office. Of course, with the money I'd received off that last job, I could do better, much better.

I proceeded over to my desk and checked out the answering machine… Four calls. Turned it on before I went back to get my coffee, came back, and sat at my desk and looked out the window to the street below. There were always cars and people because of the coffee shop and being on a corner. Good place for my business; that was another reason I liked it there. My window from the outside read "Frederick Dumas, Investigations." The sign was also on the door leading into my office.

Call number one said, "Mr. Dumas, this is Blaine and Associates. We didn't receive your check this month for your rent. We know it had to be a mix-up or something; you are usually on time with your payments. If this message reaches you and you previously paid, please disregard.

Call number two said, "Mr. Dumas, this is Mr. Wynn. Just wanted to tell you again about the fine job you did getting my little girl back. I hope the check I sent you was satisfactory."

Call number three said, "Dumas, this is Ryan down at Ryan's Car Lot. I've got a nice convertible I'd like to put you in. Give me a call.

Call number four said, "Mr. Dumas, this is John Lewis. I work for Edwards Pharmaceutical. I heard you did some work for a few friends of mine and wanted to know if I could employ you for a job. Let me know if you're interested. We'll set up a meeting. My number is 756-8869, extension 42. Looking to hear from you."

Chapter Nine

I checked the news on my computer and saw nothing at all about the girls being released. *I guess they want to keep it quiet. No news about the other three. If they were recaptured, there wouldn't be.*

I wonder what the captain and the rest of the crew are saying, and Ms. Edwards. I'll bet she had something to do with those girls. I'll also bet my name is mud with all of them.

The rent. I think I'll pay those people six months to get them off my ass. When the first of the month comes, they want their money.

This guy, Lewis, wonder what kind of job he has for me? Must have gotten my name from Mr. Wynn or Mrs. Stone, because I don't advertise, nor am I in the Yellow Pages. I won't call him today; I'm taking today off. I checked my bank account, and it was looking damn good after I gave the girl's parents my account number. They deposited the money right away. Money people don't fuck around, and I like that.

The thing about Miami is you're never too far from the beach, and that's where I headed. Got my cooler and blanket, took out a few beers, a pint of vodka, and a couple of sandwiches, and called a cab.

The lovelies were all there; they always were on Miami Beach. Some of the most beautiful women in the world come to the beach. I found myself an umbrella, spread my blanket out, set my cooler down, took a beer out, and commenced to woman watch.

Some had the traditional swimsuits; others were almost bare-bones, the latest being G-strings. Some had no tops on at all. Since this was Miami Beach, I would say most were from Cuba, and then there were the Jamaicans, and then there were Blacks, and then there were Whites that looked Black. They all had their tans on. By nine that night, I had one of those lovelies lying beside me on my blanket, a Jamaican beauty who hardly spoke any English, but I'll have to say this, we managed.

It's funny about making love on the beach; no one gives a damn. It's like live and let live. Of course, after a while, when we were getting into it, we never noticed the people anyway.

About midnight, the girl went her way, and I called a cab and went home. No long-term romance for us; she'd gotten what she wanted, and I'd surely gotten what I needed. Everybody was happy.

I hadn't thought about Teresa all day.

I called Mr. Lewis the next day, and we set up an appointment at his office for the following afternoon at two. Before I got there, I stopped at a taco stand and bought two tacos and a Coke. Walked across the street and into his building. Since it was only one thirty-five, I sat in the lobby till ten till. The building was about ten stories high, large fountain out front with the water flowing out in a spray. Coming from the street, you had to walk around it to get into the building. Ten till, I went to the elevator and up to the top floor. Once there, I didn't have to look for a room number because they had the whole floor. In the middle of the room, across from the elevator, was a reception desk, if you want to call it that. It was large and circular, and right in the middle, in a high chair looking down on everyone who came by, was one of the blackest women I had ever seen, and I'd seen a few. Jamaican, I think. Black shoulder-length hair, long, rounded earrings, a solid gold chain around her neck. Shoulder-less top, small tattoo over her right breast of a robin. She looked like a damn Amazon, and I had to look up at her until I realized why she was so tall. She was sitting on a platform and looking down. Don't know why they had something like that, but it sure was impressive. I looked around the place and noticed that the whole area was in the glass. Damn impressive.

I walked up to the desk at one fifty-seven and told the receptionist who I was, and she said "Yes, Mr. Dumas, Mr. Lewis is expecting you. His office is straight back and to the right." I thanked her and followed her directions. I swear she had a smile that would turn the night into day, the rain into sunshine, and a cloudy day sunny.

When I got to Mr. Lewis's office, I had a spring in my step. Mr. Lewis was a short man of say fifty-two years, five foot two and bald headed, clean shaven, wearing a three-piece pinstripe suit with a gold chain hanging down from his vest watch pocket. A Rolex watch was on his wrist, and three of the largest diamond rings I had ever seen on his fingers. His pinky held the largest. In my old neighborhood, they'd kill for something like that.

"Mr. Dumas, I hope you didn't have any trouble finding the place?"

I said, "I didn't."

"Could I offer you something to drink?" he said.

"Water will do fine," I said. Even though I could have used something stronger, but on the first meeting, I didn't want him to think I was an alcoholic.

"I've been hearing good things about you, Mr. Dumas. Are they true?"

"It depends on what you heard, Mr. Lewis."

"I heard you go all out to get the job done, and I also heard about the girls you rescued. I like that. And you are very discreet with what you do. If that's true, you may be the man I need to handle this problem I have."

"And what problem would that be, Mr. Lewis?"

Chapter Ten

Meanwhile, across the water.

"How did it go, Captain?" Seymour said.

"Better than I expected, but they were still pissed off. The only good thing is they hadn't paid us for the merchandise yet and they hadn't seen the girls. They're into blondes, and they were all blondes except the China doll. Ms. Edmonds picked her, said she was a sure thing and that the Arabians would love her. They did give me some advice: if I make another contract with them in the future, I'd better deliver, money paid or not."

"So, what's the plan now, Captain?"

"To pick up and deliver our cargo as usual, and get back to Miami and finish our business with Mr. Dumas. You wouldn't know anyone there who could handle that for us, do you?"

"I do, Captain, but they want to see their money up front. These guys don't trust anybody."

"You know, we could take care of him ourselves. We'll be in port about five days before we have to sail out again. First, though, we must locate him. You think your people can do that?"

"I'm sure they can, Captain. Anything you won't."

"Look, Seymour, let's do this. Have your people find him, and you and I will do the job ourselves. We owe him, and I'd like to pay him back personally. What's the word from the crew? How do they feel about this?"

"They want a piece of him themselves. They had already spent their share."

"We're going to need more girls when we get back. Maybe we can hold on to these. While we're out on the water, make your call and arrange it."

"You plan on giving the men leave time while we're here?"

"Why not? We have nothing left to protect. Leave a skeleton crew and let the others go. We'll be leaving in three to five days. We should be loaded up by then."

"What about our passengers, Captain? We still have three."

"No change. They are just continuing the trip with us and will return to Miami. After all, they don't know what's going on except we lost two passengers, who they think just left the ship because they like the area where they were. It happens. They know nothing about the girls and what went down."

"You know, Captain, I was just thinking. I could fly back, take care of Dumas, and have the girls ready for our next trip. We're only going to have a little over a week to find Dumas and get the girls ready. That's hardly enough time."

"Seymour, you're my first mate, and I'd be lost without you. Let me think on it. And by the way, we will need a new benefactor."

"How was your trip, Ms. Edmonds?"

"I wish you hadn't asked me that, Ted. To tell you the truth, it all went bad. And I blame it all on the captain. If he'd been taking care of his job, this never would have happened."

"Tell me what happened."

"All you need to know is that the girls are gone and so is our money. And I blame it all on the captain."

"You going to let it go or what?"

"No, I'm not letting it go. I can't do that. I can't let him get away with that. I just can't. If the Arabs don't do him, then I will. He'll be back in a few weeks, and that's when it'll happen."

Chapter Eleven

Later…

"Did you make up your mind?"

"Yes, I think so. Get your people together and be ready to go."

"Do you have any special way you want him dead?"

"Yes, I do, Ted. Yes, I do."

"You think we'll have any problems finding another ship and captain?"

"I've had my eye on this other ship, and I've heard good things about its captain. Should have gone with him from the start."

"So, we're going to stay with abducting girls?"

"Ted, there's just too much money in this business to stop. I can't do that. I'll speak to the captain of our new ship, the Soul. You start looking for more girls. Remember, all must be young, blue-eyed, and blond."

Two days after I talked to Mr. Lewis, I was on my way to Germany to find another lost kid, although this time it was of her own choosing. Her parents didn't know for sure, but they'd felt something was wrong. I'd told them that I thought they were just spending their money when there was no need for it, in my opinion. They'd informed me that it was their money, and do I want the job?

What the hell, I'd thought, *at least I get a free trip to Germany*.

I arrived in Frankfurt at three thirty that afternoon and had the taxi driver take me to a local hotel. I didn't much worry about the price because Mr. Lewis was paying. Once in the room, I looked in the fridge and took out a couple of bottles of vodka that every hotel seems to keep for their guests, for a price. Every bottle you drank was put on your bill. There must have been at least twenty-five bottles of all kinds in there, and beer, German and American.

After I got settled, at six, I went down to the restaurant to eat. The place was a nice size, and I guess I arrived around supper time because I had to wait for a table. If I had known this, I would have had dinner sent up to my room, but that's the way it goes. It used to be the same way when I was in the military, hurry up and wait. I finally got my table after a couple of drinks. The dinner was quite good, a little different from the States. After dinner, I walked around to get a better understanding of the place. After all, it was quite large, with three to four lounges and two large restaurants. It was thirty-five stories high, with a lounge at the very top, and my suite was 422. After a few more drinks, I headed back to my suite.

I spotted it as I was going to the bathroom: my bags had been moved. I mean, they were still on my bed, but not the way I remembered them. On further inspection, I found that someone had gone through them. I didn't have much of anything; my .38 I couldn't get on the plane with me, and my derringer I carried in a secret compartment that I checked, but there was my passport. They'd left that, but it had been moved. There were my notes on Lewis's daughter and where she might be. *Hell, I just got into town, how did they get on to me so fast? What has this girl gotten herself into?*

Meanwhile, back in Miami, Seymour had convinced the captain to let him fly back to set up more girls to transport and to take care of Dumas. He located Dumas's office, broke in, and started going through his stuff. He located the door to his apartment and entered and started searching. Eventually he came across flight information to Germany, round-trip to Frankfurt with no return date. Seymour listened to the answering machine, which had three calls.

Number one said, "Dumas, this is Carl down at JK Cadillac. I still have that convertible. Just waiting on your signature. Come by."

Number two: "Dumas, this is Sarah. I haven't heard from you. Call me."

Number three: "Mr. Dumas, I have a job for you if you have the time. My number's on your machine. My name's Demon."

Seymour locked the door on his way out. He thought that it looked like Dumas wouldn't be back in town for a while. Maybe the captain would be in by that time.

Seymour's next move was to find a donor for the girls, eight to ten of them, blonde, blue eyes. He had an idea of where to look and maybe a deal like they'd had before. He was due to meet with an individual who could set it all up. Seymour would do what he could, and when the captain got there, he would finalize the deal.

One thing I hate about going to another country is the language. I can't speak German. The next would be the money. The only thing I know about German money is that a mark is like our quarter, so four marks would be an American dollar. Five marks (and they do have a coin like that) is a dollar twenty-five. And twenty marks is five dollars. And on and on like that. I managed to learn a few words like "ish liable dish," which means "I love you." Thank you and good morning. Thankfully, a lot of the Germans can speak English. So, as you would have guessed, my wallet was full of twenty-mark notes.

Mr. Lewis had told me where his daughter might be, so the next day, I headed for number three Am Hof Street. It was a quiet little place in a very secluded neighborhood, with even a little white picket fence; unbelievable. When the taxi drove up, I noticed that the streets were absent of any traffic. I quizzed the driver and asked him what was going on. All he said was, "Oktoberfest." People go early and stay late.

"Do you want me to wait?" he asked.

"Looks like no one's home to me, so you had better wait," I said.

I opened the gate and walked up to the door, knocked once, and the door open. I pushed it in farther and announced my presence. I stepped in and called out again, "Is anyone home?"

Left of the foyer was what looked like the front room, and lying there on the floor were two bodies, one male and one female. On further inspection, I recognized the female as Alberta, Lewis's daughter. The male I didn't know. I took out my cell phone and took a picture of both. They both had been shot at least once in the head. Someone had wanted them dead for real.

I took another ten minutes to search the place. Near the bodies, I found a cufflink with the Eiffel Tower on it, which I stuck in my pocket. Also, there was one .32 caliber casing that I guess the killers had missed. I left that there for the police.

Three glasses were on the table, which led me to believe there had been only one killer, but there may have been two. I searched the dead man's wallet and found his name was Ralf Hammer. He also had about 1200 marks. I took that.

Alberta's purse held the usual women stuff, plus a few personal cards and 300 marks. I also took that. I looked around to see what I'd missed. I knew I'd missed something, but time was of the essence. Maybe the cards and things I taken from both would tell me something later, although I'd only been hired to find Alberta and I'd done that.

Back in the taxi, the driver asked me if I'd found who I was looking for. I told him I had but that they couldn't talk right then.

I called my employer and informed him of what I had found, the death of his daughter. He wasn't happy at all, even though he said they weren't too close. He asked me, "Are you sure?" I sent him the pictures of her and the male beside her. He was very quiet for a while, and then he asked me if I had any idea who'd done it. I said that I didn't.

"Could you find out?" he asked me.

" I could try," I said.

"When you do," he said, "send them on the same trip as my daughter. And Mr. Dumas, if you do this for me, you'll be able to retire."

Chapter Twelve

Two weeks later, the Bertha docked in the Miami port. Seymour was there. He met with Captain Akins, who asked, "Were you able to get everything accomplished?"

"I did, Captain. I met the contact for the girls, and we've got eight of them ready to go. All you need to do is meet up with them and finalize the deal. I never could catch up with Dumas. He's out of the country, but he may be back by now. We can check him out while you're here. I know where he lives. You'll get the chance to do him yourself."

"Sounds good to me, Seymour. You did a good job. When do we meet with the people who have the merchandise?"

"Two nights from now," Seymour said.

"That's excellent. We'll be in port for a little over a week."

The next night, Seymour and the captain made it over to Dumas's place. Both had acquired more automatic pistols. Now Seymour had two. They entered Dumas's office the same way Seymour had earlier. Nothing had changed; Dumas still wasn't back. After searching the place again, Seymour sat down at the desk, looked through the drawers, and found half a bottle of vodka. He smelled it, took a drink right from the bottle, and then said to the captain, "What now?"

"We have another week we can wait, and then we must be on our way. I sure hate to miss Dumas, but the job comes first. We'll just have to catch him another time. But we're just like the elephant. We never forget."

The next night, at approximately ten forty-five, the captain and Seymour met up with the people with the girls, two of them. They asked him if he had the money.

The captain informed them that he'd been unable to find a backer but he had half the money. Maybe they could make a deal?

The contact told the captain he was not able to make a deal like that; he'd have to go through his boss. "You'll want to see the girls anyway, so I'll call, and we'll meet with them."

"Sounds good to me," the captain said. "Let's go."

The contact, who was actually Ms. Edmonds man Ted, got on his cellphone and said, "We're on our way."

They drove ten miles out of town, to an old abandoned road with a boathouse right next to a warehouse. Ted drove his car, and the captain and Seymour followed in theirs.

"They're not too worried about us knowing where they've got the girls," Seymour said. "They must be going to move locations after they turn them over to us."

"Who cares," the captain said. "If we can make this deal, then we'll be partners. But they did find a place far out."

"Look out there," Seymour said. "Is that an alligator I see?"

Ted had gotten out of his car, and he motioned for Seymour and the captain to follow. Once inside the warehouse, Ted walked to the center of the floor. Seymour and the captain followed.

Once there, three spotlights went on and pointed at them.

"What the hell?" the captain said. "What is this?"

Ted turned around, and he had a 38 pistol in his hand. To someone out of sight, he said, "Search them."

Two men came out the shadows and began patting captain and Seymour down. They came up with the three weapons plus a couple of pocket knives. They put the two captives' hands behind their backs and tied them with plastic strips. Then they threw them down on the floor and tied their feet together with more plastic strips.

"What is this all about?" the captain asked. "Whatever it is, I'm sure we can work it out."

"What, man? We didn't do anything to you. Let us go," Seymour said.

"It'll go easier on you if you just shut the fuck up," Ted said.

"Look," the captain said, "whatever you are getting paid for this, I'll double it."

"Didn't I tell you to shut the fuck up?" Ted said. He pulled a chair up and sat down and waited. The others faded into the background.

Twenty minutes later, the door opened and what sounded like someone in high heels walked across the floor and into the light. "Hello, Captain," Ms. Edmonds said.

The captain's eyes shot wide in surprise, and his mouth dropped open. Seymour said, "Ms. Edmonds, can you tell us what this is all about? Can you get us out of this?"

"Seymour," the captain said, "I don't think Ms. Edmonds is here to get us out of anything. She's the one who put us into this mess. Why are we here, Ms. Edmonds? Is it about the girls, the money?"

"It's always been about the money, Captain. I thought the Arabs would have done you in and saved me the trouble. Answer me one question, Captain? Do you have my money?"

"I don't have any money like that. You know that," the captain said.

"Well, it looks like we've wasted both our time."

"You plan to kill us, Ms. Edmonds. Is that what you plan to do?"

"Your damn right, Captain. What did you expect?"

"Look," said Seymour, "why don't you go after Dumas? He's the cause of all this. He took the girls."

"I'll tell you what I'm going to do, Seymour. I'm going to kill you quick. After all, I realize you're only the first mate, but there is always collateral damage, and looks like you're it. Now, enough talk! Ted, give me your gun."

"Wait a minute, Ms. Edmonds. Don't do this," Seymour begged.

Edmonds shot him in the head. "You see," she said. "I'm a woman of my word," and then she shot the captain in his right leg. He screamed and grabbed at his leg.

"Captain, I've got something special for you. Ted, take him out to Goliath."

"Goliath, who is Goliath?" the captain asked.

Ted's two men picked the captain up by his arms and walked him out back to the boat ramp. They took him out on the deck, and one picked up an oar and beat the water with it. From out of nowhere came the largest alligator the captain had ever seen. It had to have been at least thirty feet long and weighed over a ton. The men attempted to throw the captain into the water, and he resisted as best he could. When he saw he was losing the battle, he screamed and pleaded for his life.

After being thrown into the water, the gator was on him. Goliath grabbed him by the head and swam away, the captain screaming all the while, and then he vanished beneath the water. Seymour was brought out and tossed into the water right behind the captain.

"Goliath won't need to be fed for a month now," one of the men said.

"Who is this Dumas guy the captain was talking about?" Ted asked. "Do we need to serve him up to Goliath too?"

"I don't know, Ted," said Ms. Edmonds. "I must think about that one. He did take the girls, but the captain should have protected them better than he did. Dumas! We'll see."

Chapter Thirteen

Meanwhile, in Frankfurt, Dumas was looking over the papers he had taken from the two dead people. One was a business card from the Cairo Electric Company, Douglas Friedman, general manager. The second was a card with the name JT Rowlands on it and a phone number. There was a plain piece of paper folded up with a phone number and the words "Call me ASAP." The note had no name on it.

The cufflink, now who could that belong to? Maybe left by the killer. I picked up the phone and dialed the number on the note. The person who answered was reluctant to speak until I told him who I was and that Alberta was dead. He agreed to meet with me.

I met Jon at the Bon-Hoff train station at the concession stand. He had described himself to me as wearing a yellow ribbon in his coat label. I almost missed him because of what else he was wearing. Sitting at one of the tables near the window was an African about twenty-five years old, five foot five, 140 pounds. Red shoes, green pants, yellow shirt, purple sports coat with yellow flowers on it. Green and yellow tie. Africans never could dress, not like the brothers back in the states. There's a lot of difference between them and us; I guess the way we dress is just one of them.

"Jon?" I said, sitting down at his table.

"Yes, Dumas? Tell me about Alberta and Ralph. You say they're dead?"

I showed him the pictures of both.

"Damn," he said. "I tried to warn them what was coming, twice. The last time, I slipped a note underneath their door."

"You said you tried to warn them twice. When was the first time?"

"I tried calling them but didn't get any answer. That was the first time."

"What's this all about, Jon, and who is Ralph?"

"Ralph was Jenny's old man, and they were both strung out on heroin. The people that they were dealing with didn't know this. They were given a batch of drugs to sell, and what they did was sell some and consume the rest. The people wanted their money or their asses. It looks like they got their asses."

"Where do you come in, Jon? What's your stake in all this?"

"I was helping them sell the drugs and taking a little for myself, but they caught us. They tried to hit me first, but I got away and tried to notify them but never could. I thought you were Ralph and Jenny trying to get back to me. Now I'm going to have to start running."

"Do you know why someone would want to search my room?"

"Jenny told me once that her father was trying to locate her and that he wasn't above sending someone over to see what she was doing. They may have been monitoring her calls. If I was you, I'd watch my ass. They may think you were in on it with her. Look, I got to make tracks. I'm sure I'm next on their list."

After Jon left, I stayed there at the table, finishing my beer, wondering where to go from there, when I heard all kinds of emergency lights going off and people running toward the tracks. I had a bad feeling come over me, and I got up and began walking toward the crowd. I made my way through to the front and saw Jon lying below on the tracks like a Christmas tree in October, blood coming out of a small hole in his temple.

Well, that's number three, I thought. *Jon's the last one unless they decide to come after me.*

Back in the hotel room, I went over the few clues I had left: two business cards and one cufflink. I started with the card that had the address on it, Cairo Electric Company. Douglas Ferdinand, general manager.

The cab let me out on the Biden Strassen right in front of the Gunstock Building, which housed the Cairo Electric Company. The company was on the fourth floor of the four-story building. I walked into the building and up to the information desk and was directed to the elevator and the fourth floor. There was another receptionist at a desk there who asked me who I was there to see and if I had an appointment. I told her who I was there to see and that no, I had no appointment. She contacted Mr. Ferdinand's office, and he told her he didn't know me and had no appointment with me. I told the secretary that I wanted to talk to him about a young lady named Alberta Lewis, who was murdered. The secretary passed on what I'd told her, and Mr. Ferdinand told her to send me on back.

Standing up beside a very large desk and office chair was Mr. Ferdinand, a very tall man of about six foot six and over 250 pounds, approximately fifty-eight years old, blonde, and with a clean-shaven face. Three-piece pinstripe suit, gold watch chain in his vest pocket, a cigar sticking out the left side of his month.

"Mr. Dumas, you mentioned something about Alberta Lewis being dead. Are you the police?"

"No, sir, I'm not, but I know of her death, and I'm checking around to see if I can find out her last locations. Maybe I can find out who killed her."

"If you are not the police, then who are you representing?"

"I'm representing her father. He asked me to look into her death. What can you tell me?"

"Alberta worked here for six months, but I had to let her go because of drugs. She was doing fine until she met up with some guy, and then she started coming to work late, if at all. When she did come in, she was often high. I liked Alberta. I hated to let her go. How did she die?"

"She was murdered," I said.

"That's about all I can tell you, except I did get a call from the Rayon Company, which is a drug company, for a reference. Against my better judgment, I gave her an acceptable one."

"Do you happen to have their address and phone number? And by the way, do you know the person Alberta took up with?"

He gave me the address and phone number of the Rayon Company. "The guy Alberta took up with was named Ralph Makin. He worked here too. We also had to let him go."

After I departed the Gunstock Building, I stopped at a café bar for a beer. Once there, and while drinking my beer, I pulled out the address Ferdinand had given me. I also pulled out the two other business cards I had. The one with no address and just the phone number had the same number as the Rayon Company. I pulled my phone out and called the number, and the answering service came on and said that the Rayon Company was closed. The hours of operation were between eight am to five pm, Monday through Friday. This was Wednesday, and I made it a point to be there the next morning.

Chapter Fourteen

Eight that night, I was in the hotel dining room having a stack, medium rare. A vodka cocktail and I were feeling good. I made it over to the bar adjacent to the dining room to see if I might catch me a little cutie for the night. Since this was a Wednesday, the pickings were light. I did spot one pretty sitting at the bar, skirt halfway up her thighs, high heels with a gold ankle bracelet. A light pullover sweater with a beret on her head. The lips, I was really attracted to her lips, which were large and voluptuous. I could imagine those lips wrapped around…

The sweater also showed off her breasts, which were somewhere in the high thirties and low forties. After observing all that, I noticed that she was looking back at me. Before I could make my move, the waitress came over and set a vodka on the rocks on my table and said, "It's from the lady at the bar." I looked over at her and held up my drink in a toast. Two minutes later, I was out of my seat and over at the bar, sitting next to her. I thanked her for the drink and asked her name.

"Jeanette," she said. "And what's yours?"

"Frederick Dumas," I said. "You can call me Dumas."

One thing led to another, the usual bullshit you talk about with a new pickup, and eventually I said, "I have a room here at the hotel. Maybe we can go there and finish our drink?"

She looked at me and said," Dumas, I hate to hit you with this, but I usually get paid for what you are wanting to do."

I looked at her, I mean all of her, and said, "I'll have to tell you, Jeanette, it's been a long time since I had to pay for sex, not since Vietnam." I looked at her again and said. "How much are we talking about?"

She leaned over and whispered in my ear, and I said, "Let's go."

I walked in the room first, and something hit me. I hit the floor, and I heard someone tell Jeanette to get lost. There were at least two of them, maybe three. They worked me over good, mostly kicking me in the ribs, and they didn't forget about my head. My nose felt broken. As I was lying in the middle of the floor, bleeding, one of the guys leaned over me and advised me to stop doing what I was doing and to go back to the States, and he told me that this was the last warning I'd get.

While he was leaning over me, the light showed off his tie pin... An Eiffel Tower.

At two that next morning, I woke up, pulled myself off the floor, went into the bathroom, and looked in the mirror. I didn't look so swell. The left eye had closed, and my nose was pointing south, but it had stopped bleeding. My lip was fatter than usual, and my ribs were sore as hell, but I didn't think they were broken. I threw some water on my face, picked up a towel, and went to the fridge for some ice. Put ice cubes in the towel and lay on the bed with the towel to my face.

At nine am, I called for breakfast and had it sent up. The waiter did a double take at me and said, "Sir, we have a doctor on call at the hotel if you need one."

"I'll be all right" I said. "But it looks like I won't be going to the Rayon Company this morning."

The Rayon Company was a 10,000-square-foot warehouse on five acres fenced-in land on the outskirts of town. Alex Goring, the CEO, was sitting in his office, talking to Felix, his associate, on the phone. "Did you take care of that Dumas fellow?"

"We did and gave him a message that if he follows, he'll get out of Germany alive. We know he talked to Jon but don't know what Jon told him. Maybe the beating will convince him to leave town. I think we should have killed him."

"I told you, since he's from the States, we can't do that, just yet that is. That would bring too much heat down on us. Did you find someone to replace Alberta and Ralph?"

"I'm working on it."

"I need you and Edgar to pick up that shipment that's coming in at the dock tonight. I've got other people picking it up early tomorrow morning."

Dumas! Alex thought. *Maybe I should have let Felix kill him. If, for some reason, he doesn't leave town, we're going to have to kill him anyway. How much does he know? How much did Jon tell him?*

Alex was really having second thoughts about him. He'd see.

Saturday, I was feeling much better, and I stayed in my room all day and soaked in a hot bath for a couple of hours. Ice packs on my face, brought the swelling down somewhat. My nose moved back into place, and my lip went down. My eye was still half closed, but the swelling was not that bad. I had my food sent up to me and had them restock the bar.

I figured I'd stay in the hotel another couple of days and then, first thing Monday morning, visit the Rayon Company.

Chapter Fifteen

Monday morning, I was dropped off at the gate of the Rayon Company. For a supposedly large company, it looked rather dead. It had three cargo doors for loading and unloading, but only one lift truck was there. The gate was open, so I walked in, and while doing so, I looked around. The only thing in the warehouse was a few boxes and pallets and one old forklift that looked as though it'd never been used. The truck looked like it had a little time on it too. Other than that, it seemed as though no one was around, so I headed for what looked like the office.

One person was sitting at an ancient desk that had seen better days, on an old chair next to a file cabinet. "Can I help you?" the man asked.

"Yes," I said. "Is this the Rayon Company?"

"That's what the sign says."

"The reason I asked, looked like the place is vacant."

"We're in the process of moving," the man said. "Now, how can I help you?"

"I need to speak to someone who can tell me about on ex-employee of yours, one Alberta Lewis."

The man looked at me and said, "You want to talk to the CEO of the company. Mr. Goring. Who should I say is inquiring?"

"Frederick Dumas," I said.

He got on the phone and said, " There is a Mr. Dumas here to see you." He listened for a minute and told me to go right in.

Alex Goring was a middle age man of fifty-five, though he looked more like sixty-five. Gray hair, earring in his left ear, Hitler-type mustache. Sports jacket over a pullover sweater. He didn't get up but looked at me with cold, killer eyes, and right then, I knew I was in trouble.

"Mr. Dumas, how can I help you?"

"Mr. Goring, I understand Alberta Lewis used to work for you. I don't know if you're aware, but she's dead, and I'm looking into her death."

"Are you the police, Mr. Dumas?"

"No, I'm not. I'm a private detective from the States and looking into her death on behalf of the family."

"I see," said Goring. "Well, the only thing I could tell you is she only worked here for a few months and then she quit, just like that. She didn't even give me notice. She didn't even come back for her check."

"What type of work was she doing?"

"She was a distributor. We're in the electric business. She would go around and take orders."

"You say you're in the electric business, but I noticed that your warehouse is empty."

"That's right. We're in the process of moving. Most of our supplies are over at the new location."

At that moment, a man walked in the back door, saying, "Boss, I took care of…" Then he spotted me and froze and looked at Goring. Goring said to the man, "This is Mr. Dumas. He's inquiring into the death of Alberta Lewis. Mr. Dumas, this is Felix, one of my associates."

I greeted him, and right off, what caught my attention was his tie clip, an Eiffel Tower.

Felix saw where I was looking and told Goring he'd talk to him later and walked out the room.

"That's about all I can tell you, Mr. Dumas. I'm sorry," Goring said.

"Well, thanks, Mr. Goring. You help me more than you know." I reached into my inside pocket for my cellphone and mentioned to Goring about calling a cab.

Goring said, "Please, let me take care of that for you. The cab company knows us very well. I may even be able to get you a discount."

He got on his office phone. "Edgar, tell Felix to call a cab for Mr. Dumas, and he was right about ending that contract." Then, to me, he said, "Everything's done, Mr. Dumas. In a little while, you'll be out of here."

Two minutes later, Edgar and Felix came in. Felix was holding a gun.

"Stand up, Mr. Dumas," Goring said. He instructed Edgar to search me. Among other things, he found the cufflink and showed it to Felix. "You lose this?" he said.

Felix looked at it and said, "I was wondering where I lost that."

"What's this all about, Mr. Goring?" I asked.

"You know damn well what this is all about. I guess that ass kicking did you no good. You can't say we didn't give you a chance to leave town."

"Why did you have to kill Alberta and Ralph?" I said.

"I don't know why you need to know that, but since you won't be around that much longer, I'll tell you. They got greedy. They weren't satisfied with what we were paying them. They had to start using the product, and they had that little showboat African to help them."

"Let me guess," I said. "So you had Edgar and Felix knock them off?"

"You got that right, Dumas. We were willing to let you run, but you didn't take the hint. Wasn't getting your ass beaten enough for you?"

"You fellows did make an impression on me. I guess you're right; I should have taken the hint. How about if I take you up on that now?"

"You boys get Mr. Dumas out of here and make sure he's not heard from again."

Edgar grabbed me and pulled me out the door, followed by Felix with the gun. They were leading me into the warehouse when Edgar stumbled on an uneven piece of concrete. He went down, pulling me with him. While I was down on the floor, I reached for my derringer, which was in an ankle holster. The thing about a derringer, it's so small you can hide it just about anywhere, and it helps when you have a person who doesn't know how to search.

I shot Felix first because he held the gun. A derringer is small but carries a hell of a bang. Edgar was next. Since I only had two shots in the derringer, I had to make them count, so I shot him in the head.

Felix was still alive but just barely. I took his weapon, shot him again, and headed for the office of Alex Goring.

Epilogue

"Good morning, Mr. Dumas. Did I wake you?"

Ms. Edmonds was sitting across from me at the foot of my bed, holding a Beretta with a silencer on it. I wiped the sleep out of my eyes and started to get up, and she said, "Don't bother."

"Ms. Edmonds. Never thought I'd see you again."

"You wouldn't have, Mr. Dumas, if you hadn't taken my merchandise. You do know you must pay for that?"

"Ms. Edmonds, I was just doing a job, plus I didn't know you had anything to do with those girls."

"Would that have mattered to you if you knew?"

"Look, maybe you need to see the good captain about all that. He made it possible for the girls to be taken."

"I've seen the captain, Mr. Dumas, and he's paid the ultimate price. Now it's your turn."

"Hold on a minute, Ms. Edmonds. Can't we work this out? How about if I pay you back the money you lost?"

"Have you got $10 million, Mr. Dumas? I didn't think so. If I can't have my money, then it sure would make me feel damn good to put a couple of bullets in your head. I started to have a couple of my men take care of you, but I didn't want to leave this pleasure to anyone but me."

I could see her finger starting to tighten down on the trigger, and my whole body tightened up, knowing that there wasn't a damn thing I could do about it. Right before she pulled the trigger, that's when it happened, an explosion from the coffee shop below that took out the top floor, my apartment, my bed, refrigerator, coffee pot, and everything else in that room. Ironically, the office part was left intact.

Ms. Edmonds went down with me, except I was still in my bed. Ms. Edmonds came down on a steel rod that entered her back and came out through her neck. She still held the Beretta in her hand. With the explosion came the fire. Being in bed softened my fall quite a bit, but I still had trouble getting out of there. By the time the fire department got there, I was crawling out of what was left of the front door. There were a couple more explosions before they could get the gas turned off. My office, the part that was left, was demolished, if not by the fire then by the water from the firemen.

They told me later that if it had happened during the week, there would have been many casualties. Since it didn't... there was only one female who was found dead, burned to a crisp. They couldn't understand what she was doing there since the place was closed. The gun in her hand they really couldn't understand, a mystery. The belief was that she'd started the explosion and gotten caught up in it.

When they drove me off to the hospital, I found out I was hurt worse than I thought, broken arm, a couple of broken ribs, and a broken toe. I hadn't gotten all this when I'd rescued the girls.

I found out later that my building was a total loss and that it would be torn down. *Well, there goes my office and my home, and that settles whether I stay or go.* My landlord called and offered to find me a place to stay. After all, they did have insurance.

A week later, I was discharged from the hospital. The nurse had come in with a wheelchair, which they said all people being discharged had to use. We were about to leave the room when, right then, the door opened, and in walked Teresa.

She said, "Hello, Dumas."

For three glorious months, Teresa and I lived it up, making love every step of the way. Going out to dinner, coming back and making love. Going to the beach and making love on the beach. Going back to her place and looking in that fabulous mirror. I don't think there was ever a way we didn't make love. I think we could have written a book on the subject.

Making love on the living room floor, love on the couch, love in the chairs, love in the bathroom, in the tub, on the sink and the toilet. Not to mention the kitchen sink. I had to tell a lie that I had a hospital appointment to get a break. We took trips, Jamaica, Hawaii, Paris, and Amsterdam. Anywhere she'd ever thought she wanted to go. After all, I did have the money.

At the end of one of our trips, we decided to purchase a car. I called Ryan at the car dealership and told him we'd be down to look at a few. Teresa told me to go down and pick it out and come back and surprise her. She knew she'd like whatever I chose.

I left the house at one pm the next afternoon. The cab dropped me off twenty minutes later. I met up with Ryan, and he started taking me around the lot, showing me what he had. As soon as I saw it, I knew that was the car for me, for us. Black Lexus convertible, black top, black interior, and chrome wheels. It had everything in it but the kitchen sink. Teresa would love it. An hour and a half later, I had the keys in my hand. After paying the dealer cash, I was on my way. Naturally, I had the top down, and I had to drive around the old neighborhood to show it off before I picked up Teresa. I drove by my old office; it wasn't there. That whole block was vacant. It looked like they were starting to rebuild already. The coffee shop, I felt, they would hurry up and rebuild because it had been making quite a bit of money. My office and living quarters, I wasn't too sure about. I had to see the landlord about that. Whatever they were building, I was sure it wouldn't take them long.

I'd wasted enough time running around and felt it was time now to pick up Teresa, my woman, my girl, and my love. When I reached Teresa's apartment, there had to have been at least twenty police cars in front, so many that I had to park halfway down the block. I walked the remainder of the way, wondering what could have happened. When I walked into the compound, there were police officers everywhere, questioning everyone. I looked toward Teresa's apartment and saw that the door was open and several police officers were coming and going out the door. I started running then, past the swimming pool and up the stairs, until I stopped by one of the police officers. I was raising so much hell and fighting with the police officers until someone in authority came out and demanded who I was. I told him that I was a friend of the woman who lived there. He told the police officers who were holding me to release me. I walked into the apartment, and it was like I'd never been there before. The couch, chairs, and bar were all turned over, and there was blood all over the carpet and the body of Teresa lying on the floor. I ran over to her, but before I could touch her, the police officers stopped me. She had cuts all over her body, and the one where the most blood was coming from was her throat. It was cut from ear to ear. She was lying on her back with her eyes wide open.

I ran to the bathroom and threw up and started trembling. Two tours of Vietnam, hundreds of dead bodies, killed in all kinds of situations. Heads blown off, bodies mutilated, pregnant women's stomachs cut open and their babies taken out and played with like a football. Men's intestines pulled out and stretched as far as they could go – you'd be surprised how far your intestines will stretch. The Vietcong were something else, and we were no better. Burning up people's villages, and whoever was inside, "tough shit." We're not talking about the rapes, and both sides did that. War is a motherfucker, open season, and the ones with the biggest guns get the spoils. Not to mention the kids, that was the hardest part of all. The grownups were just par for the course, but the kids hit me the worst, but even they were nothing like this, nothing like this. Teresa and I had made plans. She'd turned out to be my best friend and surely my lover, and I'd believed she would have been my wife. Now that was all gone.

A police officer came and got me and walked me out to the balcony. Ten to fifteen minutes later, I had recovered and was asked questions about who I was and my relationship with the deceased. After answering all his questions, I asked him one: "Who could have done this and in the middle of the day?"

"All I can tell you, Mr. Dumas, is three Caucasian men came in here at approximately five pm, past the swimming pool, directly to her door, and broke in. They only stayed there ten to fifteen minutes. They taped her mouth so no one heard her screaming. They were looking for something or someone. Could that someone have been you, Mr. Dumas?"

After the police turned me loose, I returned to the Lexus and drove away. I didn't know where I was going; I was just driving. The new car I was so proud of didn't matter, not now. Nothing seemed to matter. The plans Teresa and I had made were all gone; the love we shared was gone. *What's next for me now? I have no future. My future died with Teresa.* Then I thought about Teresa lying there all cut up, bleeding, eyes wide open and legs spread apart. Beautiful, lovely Teresa.

Then I got mad, and I remembered the police officer saying, "Were they looking for you, Mr. Dumas?" And then I remembered what Ms. Edmonds had said. "I was going to have my men do you, but I decided to have that pleasure myself." It couldn't have been the captain, because Ms. Edmonds had just about admitted to me that he was dead. Now Ms. Edmond was dead, and that left only her men. The police believed there were at least two of them, maybe three. Regardless, they're dead men.

For Teresa, for me, and for love.

Other books by this author:

Enlisted at 14: A Memoir
Enlisted at 14: And the Journey Continues
Enlisted at 14: Looking Back
Willow: A Novel
Willow: One for the Team
Willow: And the Medusa
Little Miss Willow: A Short Story
Assassin
Blacker the Berry
Meet Ruben Kane
R.K. {Ruben Kane}
Ruben's Bag
Ruben's Bad Side
Smooth: A Ruben Kane Novel
Mo Kane
Here 'Tis
And Then Some
Dear Client
Ducks in a Row
Just a Dream
Dream Catcher
Beyond the Curve
First One In

Switch